# SAVING JOE LOUIS

## Isabel Marvin

*Illustrations by*
*Clovis Brown*

Published by: LMH Publishing Limited
7 Norman Road,
LOJ Industrial Complex
Suite 10-11
Kingston C.S.O., Jamaica
Tel: 876-938-0005; 938-0712
Fax: 876-759-8752
Email: lmhbookpublishing@cwjamaica.com
Website: www.lmhpublishing.com

Printed in China

ISBN: 976-610-233-3
ISBN 13: 978-976-610-171-8

**O**mar lived in Jamaica with his father, Roy, and his mother, Emily. They lived in a tiny house next door to a big house where tourists stayed in the winter.

**W**hen Roy worked for the tourists, Omar went with him. He walked behind Roy and carried a tool also. Roy laughed at this. The tourists always said, "Hello, Omar. How are you?" But Omar never answered. In fact, Omar did not speak at all.

**S**ometimes Roy became angry with his son.

"Why don't you talk, Omar? You're supposed to talk when you are four."

Omar stared at Roy but said nothing.

"He must talk so that he can go to beginners' school," Roy told Emily as she cooked the tourists' dinner one day.

**E**mily tried. She told him stories like "The Three Bears," but Omar only giggled. She sang, "Go to bed, my little Piggywig," but Omar only hummed.

**W**hen Roy walked down the hill to the store or the post office, Omar ran behind him.  They passed the beginners' school, and Omar watched the children play. They sang, "Ring Around the Rosy," and skipped in a circle.  It looked like great fun, but still he did not say anything.

**N**o one knew why Omar did not talk. Perhaps he did not need to speak. When he was hungry, his mother fed him. When he was sleepy, she put him to bed.

The doctor told Roy and Emily that Omar would talk when he was ready.

"Omar is not sick," the doctor said. "Perhaps if he played with other children, he could begin to talk."

**O**mar played with someone every day. It was not a boy, and it was not a girl.

Omar's best friend was a rooster named Joe Louis.

Sometimes Omar pretended to be a rooster too. He clucked like Joe Louis. He walked like Joe Louis. The rooster crowed loudly then.

**E**mily was angry when Joe Louis crowed, especially early in the morning when he woke the tourists. She chased the big rooster with her broom to keep him away from the big house and the newly-planted garden.

**T**hen one day a terrible thing happened. Omar was playing in the drips from the outside faucet. Joe Louis was stealing tiny pebbles under the drip. Emily was cooking fish. The fish smelled delicious. Then Omar heard Roy say a frightening thing.

"The boss has told me to get rid of the rooster tomorrow. He bothers the tourists every day."

The water dripped. The fish sizzled in coconut oil. The rooster pecked at the small rocks. But Omar felt as if the sky had turned black. He was not sure what his father meant to do to Joe Louis, but he was afraid.

Tomorrow! Omar must make a plan. He had to save Joe Louis. That night he tried to stay awake, but he could not.

An early morning breeze blew palm leaves against the tin roof of their little house. Omar awoke. A few minutes before the sun came up, he tiptoed outside.

**H**e could not find Joe Louis anywhere. He looked under the bushes near the faucet, and all around the yard. No Joe Louis. It was already too late. Tears ran down Omar's face.

**W**ait! The cage. Could Roy have put Joe Louis up in the tree cage behind Emily's clothesline?

Omar ran as fast as he could. He stubbed his bare feet often on rocks and tree roots.

When he reached the tree, he was out of breath. He looked up at the silent cage. It was still too dark to see inside the cage.

**T**he tree was too tall. How could he climb up to the cage? There was a rock under the tree, but it was not high enough.

Then he saw his mother's laundry table. It was almost under the tree, but it was not close enough. The table held the tub where she washed the tourists' clothes by hand. For as long as he could remember, the little table had stood in the same spot like a rooted tree. Could he move it?

**H**e tugged at the table. Fear for Joe Louis gave him the strength of ten. With a mighty pull, he moved the table a few inches closer to the tree. Closer. Now it was under the cage.

**C**arefully, he stepped up on the rock, then onto the table top. He reached up and tried to open the cage door. He was sure the cage was empty. He pulled out the twig holding the cage latch. Finally he opened the door and poked his hand inside.

With a flurry of feathers, the rooster sailed out the door and fluttered to the ground. Omar's heart filled with love and happiness. He was not too late!

The boy climbed down from the table. The sky turned red behind the palm trees. That meant dawn and danger. Roy would come for the rooster as soon as it was light.

Omar looked down the path. It led to the sea. Omar had gone as far as the blue Caribbean Sea only once. That was the day his grandmother came to visit Omar and his parents.

**T**here was nothing else to do. He must save Joe Louis.

Omar walked rapidly down the path. The rooster tripped jerkily along behind him.

**H**ours later, Roy and Emily found Omar and Joe Louis looking at the big ships in the harbour. A neighbour milking goats had seen Omar leave.

"**O**mar!" Roy held him tightly and raised him high in the air. "Why did you run away? What is wrong?"

Omar put his arms around his father's neck. He was happy to see his parents, but this terrible thing could not happen.

"Don't get rid of Joe Louis," Omar begged.

His mother looked up in surprise. His father almost dropped him.

"He spoke!" Emily whispered. "Omar can talk!"

"Don't get rid of Joe Louis," Omar said again. "He's my friend."

**T**hey hugged Omar. Finally Roy put him down and smiled.

"We will buy some hens to keep Joe Louis happy, Omar. Then you and I will build a pen for all the chickens. We will put it into the woods behind our house so that the tourists cannot hear him. But you cannot run around the yard with him anymore. Do you understand?"

Omar nodded his head. Then he said softly, "Yes."

"Come along, son. It's a long way home, but you already know that, don't you?" Roy said. Then he and Emily turned and began walking back up the hill.

**O**mar clucked to Joe Louis, and the two friends began climbing the dusty path. Omar's feet were tired and bruised. He knew he would soon have to go to beginners' school because he had talked. It might not be so bad. And anyway, Joe Louis was saved!